What's a joke book's favorite meal?
Pun-cakes with a side of giggles.

CW01497565

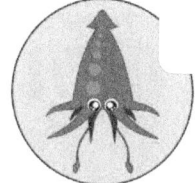

SQUARE ROOT OF SQUID PUBLISHING

BOOK CONCEPT BY: ALBERT B. SQUID
ILLUSTRATIONS/WRITING BY: ALBERT B. SQUID

JANUARY 1

My New Year's resolution is to stop making bad jokes. So far... it's snow joke how badly I'm failing.

Principal: "Why are you late?"

Student: "Because I'm not early."

Principal: "Fair enough."

Why did the astronaut break up with his girlfriend?

He needed space.

BREAKING NEWS: A giant sandwich escaped from the fridge. Police say it's on a roll.

Teacher: "Name one thing that's both smart and cool."

Student: "My brain in sunglasses."

I entered my dog into a spelling bee. He only barked once... But it was correctly spelled!

What do you call a snowman party?

A snowball!

What's a bubble's favorite kind of music?

Pop!

Knock knock.

Who's there?

Ice.

Ice who?

Ice to meet you in the new year!

Kid: "I named my pet rock Steve."

Friend: "Why Steve?"

Kid: "He just looks like a Steve."

The banana became an actor. Turns out, it slips into any role!

My goldfish started a band. They're calling themselves The Gillz.

What do you call a pile of sneezes?

Ah-chew-nami!

How do you
make a tissue
dance?

You put a little
boogie in it!

What do you call a dinosaur with an extensive vocabulary?

A thesaurus!

How do you
know when a
clown farts?

It smells funny.

I told my sock a joke. It didn't get it. Too much cotton in its ears.

What do you
call a deer with
no eyes?

No Eye Deer.

What's worse than finding a worm in your apple?

Finding half a worm!

What do singers eat before a concert?

Mic and cheese!

I asked my backpack what it wanted to be when it grows up. It said, "A jetpack, obviously."

Mom: "What happened to all the cookies?"

Me: "They mysteriously evaporated. Very scientific."

Dad: "Why is there glue in your lunchbox?"

Me: "To stick to my diet."

My little brother says he's a superhero. So far, his powers include:
1. Disappearing at cleanup time
2. Destroying all my stuff.

Why was the teacher writing on the floor?

Because it was Opposite Day and the desk was sitting in her chair!

Why did the elephant bring a suitcase to school?

Because he forgot his trunk!

Why did the crayon apply for a job?

It wanted to draw a paycheck.

My plant whispered a secret. Turns out, it's rooting for me.

I wrote a joke on my whiteboard. Now it's the pun board of education.

What do clouds wear under their raincoats?

Thunderwear!

Kid: "Do I HAVE to go to school today?"

Parent: "Yes, you're the principal."

I tried to do yoga with my dog. Now we both just lie on the floor and call it "Downward Nap."

What's yellow, slimy, and swings from the ceiling?

A booger chandelier!

What do you call
a bird who's
afraid to fly?

A chicken!

I asked the library for a book on how to disappear. They whispered, "We've never seen it return..."

My left shoe and my right shoe had an argument. Now I'm walking in circles.

I like to draw pictures of me drawing pictures of me drawing pictures...I'm going crazy!

The toaster is officially mad at me. I called it "bread's hot tub."

Kid: "My pencil is my best friend."

Parent: "Why?"

Kid: "It listens. And erases my mistakes."

What did one Valentine card say to the other?

"You make my heart skip a beat.... or maybe that's just my Wi-Fi acting up!"

If cats could vote, every law would involve naps and knocking stuff off tables.

I asked Siri to do my chores. She laughed, then scheduled a nap for herself.

Kid: "I'm practicing for the Olympics."

Friend: "In what sport?"

Kid: "Extreme chicken plucking."

My dreams are sponsored by snacks. Last night I wrestled a giant pretzel.

What did one volcano say to the other on Valentine's Day?

"I lava you!"

My socks had a dance party last night. Now they're too tired to match.

Why did the bicycle fall over?

Because it was two-tired!

My pet goldfish just published his memoir. It's called: Swim. Forget. Swim Again.

FEBRUARY 18

Kid: "What's the capital of Snacksylvania?"

Friend: "No idea."

Kid: "Cheesebite City."

Why don't books
ever get cold?

They have covers.

What is a dog's
favorite kind
of pizza?

Pup-peroni.

I entered a staring contest with my reflection. We both blinked.

Why don't aliens visit Earth anymore?

Because last time, we made them do a group project.

Knock knock.

Who's there?

Lettuce.

Lettuce who?

Lettuce in, it's freezing out here!

My backpack has a black hole. Everything I put inside disappears... except gum wrappers.

Kid: "I have a superpower."

Friend: "What is it?"

Kid: "I can hear cookies calling from the kitchen."

I wrote a rap about cleaning my room. It's called Can't Find My Floor.

What do you call a strawberry who plays guitar?

A jam session musician!

My brain at night: "Let's make a plan!" My brain in the morning: "What's a plan?"

It's my friend's birthday today, which is a leap year; he is 5 years old, but he looks 20.

Why did the peanut butter sit alone at lunch?

Because it was a little nuts!

My shoes squeaked during class. Now everyone thinks I walk in Morse code.

Why don't you iron four-leaf clovers?

Because you don't want to press your luck!

March Fourth sounds like a battle cry. That's why I declared war on laundry today.

My notebook says it's full. But I still found room for five doodles, three bad poems, and a skateboard sticker.

I joined a band made entirely of dogs. We're called The Beagles.

If vegetables could talk, broccoli would definitely be the bossy one.

I'm not messy.
I'm just
creatively
distributed.

A salesperson: "Why did you buy that computer?"

Frog: "rebate, rebate!"

What do you call a burp that turns into a sneeze, then a fart?

A triple threat.

My goldfish keeps giving me side-eye. I think he's judging me.

Why was the math book sad?

Because it had too many problems!

If a robot became a baker, would it make byte-sized cookies?

What's brown and sticky?

A stick! (Gotcha. But you were thinking of something grosser, weren't you?)

How do French
fries greet
each other?

Fry-five!

My alarm clock and I are no longer friends. We broke up over a 6:30 disagreement.

MARCH 17

I tried to catch a leprechaun. He left me a note that said, "Nice try, Rookie."

I poured cereal into the sink by mistake. Guess I'm feeding the plumbing now.

My brain took a vacation mid-homework. It sent a postcard that just said, "Nope."

Why did the banana go to the doctor?

Because it wasn't peeling well!

Kid: "What's for dinner?"

Parent: "Leftovers."

Kid: "Cool. I love eating memories."

I joined the school drama club. I'm playing "Person #4" who gets scared by a squirrel. I will be famous.

My phone autocorrected "homework" to "nopework." I feel deeply understood.

I told my dog a joke. He wagged his tail once. That's basically a standing ovation.

My pencil thinks it's better than me. Probably because it makes more good points.

What do you call a holiday where you do absolutely nothing?

A nap-tional holiday!

Kid: "Can I be in charge?"

Adult: "Of what?"

Kid: "Gravity."

My shadow has been acting suspiciously. I think it's trying to replace me.

I opened the fridge and forgot why. So I ate a pickle for emotional support.

I named my calculator "Cal." We're in a very divided relationship.

What do you call a bear with no teeth?

A gummy bear!

You: "I just saw a cat driving a car."

Friend: "No way!"

You: "Okay, fine. It was a dog in sunglasses. April Fools!"

Why did the Easter egg hide?

Because it was a little chicken!

I challenged my shadow to a race. It won. And then it mocked me the rest of the day.

What did one raindrop say to the other in April?

"I'm falling for you!"

My hamster blinked twice at me. Either he's plotting something... or he's just a really bad spy.

Why did the kid keep his belly button lint in a sandwich bag?

He was saving it for winter insulation.

The clouds looked like mashed potatoes today. I waved a fork at the sky. Just in case.

APRIL 8

I tried to write an essay. My pencil gave up first.

What do you call a sad drawing?

A blueprint.

What do you get when you microwave a diaper?

A poo-rito.

I wore socks with sandals. Now I'm legally banned from fashion magazines.

If waffles had a theme song, it'd be "Syrup Up and Dance."

What do you call a fish wearing a bowtie?

Sofishticated.

I tried being organized once. Now my mess has folders.

The school printer growled at me. I offered it paper, it wanted blood.

Why don't eggs tell jokes?

Because they might crack up!

If robots had birthdays, would they blow a fuse instead of candles?

I named my eraser "Oopsie." He knows all my secrets.

I'm not weird. I'm just built with bonus imagination."

I opened my closet. Out fell a pirate hat, six socks, and a plastic banana. Mystery: activated.

What do you get when you tickle a computer?

Giggle-bytes!

I hugged a tree today. It didn't hug back. But it leafed me a nice message.

The pencil sharpener is mad. I called it a wood vampire.

Mom: "Why is there spaghetti in your backpack?"

Kid: "It's emergency pasta. Obviously."

What do you get when a lobster takes over the TV?

Claw and Order!

My brain needs a vacation. Preferably somewhere with no math.

What's worse than stepping in dog poop barefoot?

Realizing it's not dog poop... It's yours.

My dreams are in 3D. Mostly because I fell asleep with 3 donuts.

If a crayon had a diary, it would just say: "Today I was chewed again."

I don't clean my room. I rearrange chaos into artistic zones.

I asked my brain to focus. It said, "Sorry, I only work part-time now."

I tried to do push-ups... But the floor kept pushing back.

What did the stinkbug say when it walked into a locker room?

"This place smells delicious."

My Wi-Fi went down for 5 minutes. I met my family. They seem nice.

If time flies,
then how come
Mondays take
forever?

What did the sock say to the shoe?

"I've got you covered!"

Kid: You know what?

Friend: What?

Kid: Monkey Butt.

MAY 8

What do you call a foot with no socks?

A toe-tally free spirit!

I have two
moods:
1. Motivated.
2. Marshmallow.

My imaginary friend quit today. Said I wasn't paying him enough in cookies.

My dog and I have a deal: He keeps my secrets. I pretend he didn't pee in my sister's shoes.

I gave my backpack a name: Harry. Now I have someone to blame everything on.

Teacher: "Where's your homework?"

Me: "Still in development. Like a highly anticipated sequel."

If pillows were named after a French General, they would definitely be named "Nap-oleon."

Dad: Money doesn't grow on trees.

Me: Where does it grow? And do you have a map?

Why did the principal allow Pajama Day?

Because even he wanted to wear his dinosaur onesie!

What's the best way to talk to a flower?

Just plant a few ideas!

My keyboard is mad at me. I keep hitting "escape," but it won't let me leave.

I asked my cat
for life
advice. She
blinked slowly
and knocked
over a
cup. Deep.

My brain has 324 tabs open. Only 2 are useful. The rest are memes and video game thoughts.

Why did the crab not share his dinner?

Because he is shellfish.

I joined a club called "People Who Talk to Themselves." I'm the president. And also the secretary. And also the treasurer.

I'm not
procrastinating.
I'm just giving
my future self
a challenge."

A microwave
minute is like
an hour in real
time.

If books had egos, the mystery novel would be the most dramatic.

Kid: "I cleaned my room!"

Parent: "Under the bed?"

Kid: "That's the monster's responsibility."

What do you
get when you
eat too many
baked beans?

A musical you
can't turn off.

Why did the teddy bear refuse dessert?

It was stuffed.

If I ever get stuck in a **video** game, I hope it's one I'm good at.

How do robots
eat salsa?

With computer
chips!

My brain in math class: "Let's think about penguins wearing sunglasses and skateboarding instead."

JUNE 1

(Dinosaur Day)

What do you call a dinosaur with bad eyesight?

Do-you-think-he-saurus?

If pencils ruled the world, rulers would start a rebellion.

Why did the
sun go to
school in June?

To get a little
brighter!

My big brother burped so hard, it set off the smoke alarm.

Friend: "You're weird."

You: "Thanks! Normal is boring anyway."

What's a yo-yo's favorite vegetable?

Spin-ach.

Why don't bananas ever feel lonely?

Because they hang out in bunches!

Why did the best friends start a garden?

Because they wanted their friendship to grow!

What do you call a snowman in June?

A puddle with dreams!

The vending machine and I are in a silent war. I gave it money. It gave me regret.

I tried to race
a bubble
today. I lost.
But it was a
clean defeat.

I once sneezed so hard that I scared the vacuum cleaner.

If gravity took a break, I'd finally reach the cookies on the top shelf.

What did the fart say during hide and seek?

"You can't see me, but you nose I'm here!"

I found a penny and made a wish. Now there's glitter in my cereal. I think it worked?

The spider in my bathroom has been charging me rent in stares.

Why did the paint go to the party?

Because it wanted to brush up on its social skills!

I opened the fridge and the leftover meatloaf said, "Close the door, I'm trying to rot in peace!"

Friend: "You're slow."

You: "I'm just giving you a head start!"

My calendar winked at me today. I think summer vacation is flirting.

I got hit in the head with a soda can...
It didn't hurt;
it was a soft drink.

Why was the stadium so cool?

Because it was filled with fans!

Knock knock.

Who's there?

Astro.

Astro who?

Astro-nomically funny jokes coming your way!

My friend's armpits were so stinky, the skunk said, "Respect."

I once raced a piece of toast as it popped up. Still recovering from the defeat.

What did the corn say to the butter?

"You're a-maize-ing!"

There's a sock in my drawer that hasn't seen daylight since 2022. I think it's planning a comeback tour.

Why did the computer show up late to work?

It had a hard drive.

I invented invisible ink. But I can't prove it because my notebook is blank.

If aliens ever visit Earth, I hope they don't judge us by reality shows and cheese puffs.

I challenged an ice cream cone to a staring contest. It melted under pressure.

Why did the
moon skip
dinner?

Because it was
full.

Fireflies are just bugs with built-in Wi-Fi. But it only works in the dark.

What's Uncle Sam's favorite snack?

Fire-crackers and cheese!

Sand: nature's glitter. Except it never leaves... ever.

My flip-flops
and I
fought. Now
they slap my
feet silly with
every step.

If seagulls had Instagram, it'd be 99% pics of stolen fries.

I farted in the bathtub and created a bubble so big, the rubber duck quit.

Knock knock.
Who's there?

Sandy.

Sandy who?

Sandy Claus! I'm taking a summer vacation at the beach!

I tried to build a sandcastle. It turned into a sand tragedy.

Mosquitoes: proof that even nature gets annoying updates.

Why did the dog sit in the shade?

Because he didn't want to be a hot dog!

How did the
Roman nerds
cut their hair?

With Caesars!

I waved at a dolphin. It waved back... with a splash in my face.

I wrote a poem about lemonade. It was sweet, a little sour, and made absolutely no sense.

If beach towels could talk, they'd beg for one wash a year. Just one.

Why didn't the smiley face emoji get the job?

It couldn't keep a straight face!

I tried to open a bag of chips quietly. Now I'm a one-person marching band.

I once saw a cloud shaped like a taco. It rained hot sauce 20 minutes later.

The shady tree said, "Stay cool." So I put on my sunglasses and a fake leather jacket.

Why did the booger go to school?

It wanted to get picked for the honor roll!

I tried to surf. Turns out I'm better at "falling stylishly with purpose."

Ants held a meeting on my picnic blanket. They voted me off the island.

Why was the sushi so confident?

Because it had raw talent!

My brain is solar-powered. So in winter, I just kind of buffer.

How do artists stay cool in summer?

They draw the curtains.

My cousin farted in a jar and sold it as "Grandma's Secret Recipe."

How do trees access the internet while camping?

They log in!

What do you call
an egg who's
good at sports?

An egg-cellent
athlete!

Why did the fart get expelled from school?

Because it brought backup.

I told a joke.
Nobody laughed.
Even the
crickets left.

How does a phone propose?

With a ring!

My brain tried to install an update during gym class. Now I can only do slow-motion jumping jacks.

What did the watermelon say to its crush?

You're one in a melon!

My grandfather is so old, he farts dust.

I tried to
catch some
fog
yesterday...
I mist!

What do you get when you cross a robot and a tractor?

A trans-farmer.

Why are birthdays good for your health?

Studies show that the more you have, the longer you live!

AUGUST 8 (International Cat Day)

Knock, knock.

Who's there?

Purr.

Purr who?

Purr-haps the cat hates cucumbers?

My socks formed a band. They only play toe-tally original material.

AUGUST 10

Why don't lazy people ever get lost?

Because they never go anywhere!

A bee asked to borrow my phone. Turns out it was just buzzing someone.

How do you know an elephant's been in your refrigerator?

There are footprints in the cheesecake!

Why did the scissors panic?

A lefty was coming!

What do you call a drawing of a person who is a bit strange?

A sketchy character!

A squirrel offered me a business card. He's a freelance nut accountant.

Why did the coach bring a ladder to the game?

Because he wanted the players to step up their game!

I opened a fortune cookie. It just said, "Duck!"

The cereal box gave me a riddle. I answered correctly and unlocked a portal to the refrigerator.

My towel started a podcast. It's called Dry Humor.

The elevator and I are in a complicated relationship. We both bring each other down sometimes.

Why did the triangle refuse to be friends with the circle?

Because it was pointless.

I scratched my belly button and found a popcorn kernel from the last movie night.

I told a joke so cheesy, my grilled cheese sandwich got jealous.

My rubber duck just got elected mayor of the bathtub. His first law? More bubbles, less drama.

What do you call
a crazy tick on
the moon?

A luna-tick.

I sneezed so hard, I accidentally reset my internal GPS. Now I think I live in Antarctica.

The tree was being annoying.

I said, "Leaf me alone."

It replied, "Wood you stop?"

Robot: "Get out of here!"

Bolt: "I'm like your favorite song, you can't get me out of your head."

My little brother ate a crayon, and now his poop is a rainbow.

What did the swan say when the goose farted?

"Did someone just step on a duck?"

I caught a fly trying to log into my Wi-Fi. Its

username was "BuzzBuzz123."

I only know 25 letters of the alphabet.
I don't know y.

The fan in my room spins gossip. I heard it whisper about the lamp last night.

I tried to high-five a cloud. I missed. Got a thunderclap instead.

I used to play piano by ear.

Now I use my hands.

SEPTEMBER 5 (Cheese Pizza Day)

Knock, knock.

Who's there?

Cheese.

Cheese who?

Cheese a nice pizza, isn't she?

A bird joined our math class. Turns out it's a real tweet-cher's pet.

What did the mystery meat say to the fork?

"I'm not sure what I am either..."

I'm reading a book on anti-gravity... It's impossible to put down!

I made a salad so fancy that the lettuce asked for an autograph.

Why did the baseball team bring string to the game?

To tie the score!

What's a math teacher's favorite type of tree?

A geometree

I told a joke to the ceiling. It cracked up. Literally.

What's the best thing about fall in September?

That you can finally leaf your worries behind!

I ordered a chicken and an egg online.
I'll let you know.

What do you call fake spaghetti?

An impasta.

I tried to build a robot out of spoons. But it kept stirring up trouble.

If bananas were superheroes, they'd always slip away before the villain caught them.

My pencil broke up with my eraser. Said they were "rubbing each other the wrong way."

Why was the pirate a great singer?

Because he could hit the high C!

What do you call a factory that makes okay products?

A satisfactory.

What do you call two birds stuck together?

Velcrows.

The thermometer told me to "chill." I said, "You first!"

The floor groaned when I got out of bed. Even IT wasn't ready for Monday.

My baby sister sneezed right into my cereal. Now it's called Snot-Os.

Why did the golfer bring two pairs of pants?

In case he got a hole in one.

Parallel lines
have so much in
common...
It's a shame
they'll never
meet.

The soccer ball rolled away during PE. Said it was tired of being kicked around.

If you clean a vacuum cleaner... Does that make you the vacuum cleaner?

What's orange
and sounds like
a parrot?

A carrot.

I stayed up all night reading a book on glue... I just couldn't put it down!

Why are ghosts bad at lying?

Because you can see right through them!

Halloween Poem:
The ghost gave a
spooky glance.
The kids got
poopy pants.

Why don't zombies eat clowns?

Because they taste funny.

Friend: "You're not cool."

You: "Cool is temporary. Awesome is forever."

Why did the student eat his math homework?

Because the teacher said it was a piece of cake!

The rake quit today. It said, "I can't handle this leaf drama anymore."

A ghost tried to scare me. I asked if it could haunt my homework instead.

How many tickles does it take to make an octopus laugh?

Ten tickles!

What did Frankenstein say on Halloween while picking his nose?

Flick or Eat?

My backpack groaned and said, "Stop feeding me books, I'm full.

What do you call a sleeping bull?

A bulldozer!

A candy corn called me "basic." So I challenged it to a sweetness contest. I won. Easily.

The wind stole my hat and yelled, "Freeeeeedom!"

What kind of dessert do ghosts like best?

Ice scream!

I asked a mummy how he stays so calm. He said, "I just unwind."

Knock knock.

Who's there?

Boo.

Boo who?

Don't cry, it's just a Halloween joke!

My pumpkin said it needed moisturizer. Now it's in the bathroom with a face mask on.

The scarecrow asked for a raise. He said, "I'm outstanding in my field."

Why was the basketball court wet?

Because the players dribbled all over it!

What did one raindrop say to the other?

"Two's company, three's a cloud!"

What do you call a snake who works for the government?

A civil serpent!

The ghost at school got detention. It kept booing during the spelling test.

I tried to take a selfie with a bat. Now it's my new hair accessory.

My vampire friend hates jokes about blood.
He says they're vein.

I dressed up as a burrito for Halloween. Three kids tried to dip me in salsa.

A spider moved into my pencil case. It's opened a web design business.

What do you call a llama who likes to act?

A drama-llama.

Why can't you trust atoms?

Because they make up everything!

What kind of dog does Dracula have?

A bloodhound!

What do you call
a witch who lives
at the beach?

A sand-witch!

How do you make
a skeleton laugh?

Tickle its funny
bone!

Why did the smartphone go to school?

To improve its cell-f-esteem!

What do you call a movie about vegetables?

A romaine-tic comedy!

Why didn't the sandwich make any friends?

Because it was full of baloney!

Knock knock.

Who's there?

Alpaca.

Alpaca who?

Alpaca the suitcase, you load up the car!

The mashed potatoes challenged me to a dance battle. I whipped them.

Why did the turkey join a band in November?

Because it had the drumsticks!

My friend's lunch smelled so bad that the garbage can backed away.

Why are chemists excellent at solving problems?

Because they always have the solution!

I saw a squirrel ordering pumpkin spice. It had a tiny scarf and very strong opinions.

What do you call a sleeping dinosaur?

A dino-snore.

How do onions get around town?

In a cry-sler!

What do you call
a lazy vegetable?

A couch potato!

I saw a unicorn at the mall. He was buying glitter and arguing with a gorilla over coupons.

What's a golfer's favorite type of music?

Swing!

My boots are in a relationship with a puddle. It's complicated.

Why did the pilgrim's pants always fall down?

Because they wore their belt buckle on their hat!

Knock knock.

Who's there?

Snot.

Snot who?

Snot polite to pick your nose.

Why did the painting go to jail?

Because it was framed!

Why did the toilet quit its job?

It got tired of everyone's crap.

Why did the cat wear a fancy hat?

Because it wanted to be the purr-fect fashionista.

What kind of things does a farmer talk about when milking a cow?

Udder nonsense.

I opened my notebook. It yawned louder than I did.

Why can't your nose be **12** inches long?

Because then it would be a foot.

NOVEMBER 24 (Unique Talent Day)

My friend can touch his toes with his tongue. He's always putting his foot in his mouth.

Why did the barber win the race?

Because he took a shortcut!

Did you hear about the cheese factory explosion?

There was nothing left but de-brie.

My family tried to play charades after dinner. Turns out, Dad's impression of a "microwave" is just... loud humming.

What kind of building weighs the least?

A lighthouse!

The leftover pie joined a band. Their first hit? "Crust Me, I'm Delicious."

Why did the smartphone need glasses?

Because it lost its contacts.

What kind of apple isn't an apple?

A pineapple!

Why did the kid wear sunglasses in class?

Because his future was so bright!

What's an airplane's favorite type of music?

Heavy metal!

Why did the garbage can start telling jokes?

Because it had a scent of humor

The tree ornaments held a secret meeting. I think they're planning to revolt against the tinsel.

I asked the reindeer if they liked flying. They said, "Nah. But the snacks in First Sleigh are great."

Why did the kitten sit next to the computer?

Because it wanted to keep an eye on the mouse.

What did the teacher say to the time traveler?

"Stop turning in homework before I assign it!"

The Elf on the Shelf's cousin visited from Canada. His name is the Elf from Guelph.

What do you call a fish that practices medicine?

A sturgeon.

I asked my dog what two minus two is.

He said nothing.

What's a
mermaid's
favorite subject?

Current events!

My sled refused to go downhill. It said, "I have no direction in life."

The gingerbread house asked for property insurance. You know, in case of "bite damage."

My snow globe has drama. The tiny ice skaters aren't talking to the snowman.

Knock knock.

Who's there?

Snow.

Snow who?

Snow place like home for the holidays!

Why was the Christmas tree so bad at knitting?

Because it kept dropping its needles!

DECEMBER 18

(Bake Cookies Day)

How do you know a cookie is rich?

It has lots of dough!

What do you get
if you cross a
snowman and a
dog in
December?

Frostbite!

Santa called me "technically nice." Which feels like an insult?

What did the zero say to the eight?

Nice belt!

A polar bear
offered me a
snow
cone. Spoiler: It
was just snow.

I gave a snowman a high five. His arm fell off. We're no longer on speaking terms.

What do you call Santa when he takes a break?

Santa Pause.

I opened my gift
and it
yelled, "Surprise!
I'm clothes
again!"

What's worse than a smelly gym sock?

Two smelly gym socks!

My leftovers started a band. They're called Gravy Train and the Stuffin' Muffins.

My snowman melted and left me a goodbye note. It just said: "Chill out."

The remote control disappeared again. I blame the couch monster. He's growing stronger.

I tried eating healthy after Christmas. I started with the chocolate Santa first.

Why do you need a jeweler on New Year's Eve?

To ring in the new year!

DO YOU WANT TO LEARN HOW TO DRAW COOL STUFF IN 3D? CHECK OUT THIS BOOK BY ALBERT B. SQUID!

ABOUT THE AUTHOR

ALBERT B. SQUID

If you spot this person please call our HOTLINE at 867-5309 ask for Tommy.

Born to a family of construction peeps, ALBERT B. SQUID was raised on construction sites in Massachusetts. Believe it or not, he holds two degrees in Engineering and Architecture and has worked as an Architect in Boston, Tokyo, and Seoul. In the year 2000, Squid started an independent children's book publishing company in NYC. I had fun doing that.....I mean HE (Albert B. Squid) had fun doing that! After becoming a freelance voice actor, the elusive author's whereabouts are unknown. He was last seen on a college campus in Amherst, Massachusetts talking about philosophy with a man named Mr. Black and his friend named Joe. He was heard asking "Where did my mind go?". To which Mr. Black replied "In the ocean." Kind of a strange conversation.

albertbsquid.com

Printed in Dunstable, United Kingdom

75853664R00208